TRUDY
the
Brave Donkey

LORI LANGDON

ISBN 978-1-0980-5822-7 (paperback)
ISBN 978-1-0980-6124-1 (hardcover)
ISBN 978-1-0980-5823-4 (digital)

Christian Faith Publishing, Inc.
832 Park Avenue
Meadville, PA 16335
www.christianfaithpublishing.com

Printed in the United States of America

Introduction

Welcome to Langdon farm!

We are located in rural eastern North Carolina. Our farm has dogs, bunny rabbits, barn cats, lots of children, a big garden, a herd of cows, and, of course, an adorable donkey named Trudy.

During the COVID-19 pandemic of 2020, we had a little extra time on our hands. We decided it might be fun to share with our friends some of the funny things that Trudy does. She can be downright hilarious.

Everything in this book is mostly true with a little bit of room left for imagination. We both think reading is delightful, and we hope that you enjoy this visit to our farm.

Blessings to you and your family!

Prologue

If there's one thing I know about my girl, it is that she loves reading. Even before I was born, she read a book called *Gertruda's Oath* (oath means a promise). It was a true story about a nanny in the time of World War Two. This nanny took care of a little boy whose parents were Jewish. His parents made her promise to take care of him no matter what happened. Gertruda was very brave and kept her promise. She protected the little boy and raised him as her very own son.

When my girl read that book, she decided all at the same time that she wanted a donkey and that she would name me in honor of Gertruda.

So my official name is Gertruda, but all my friends call me Trudy.

1

....

The Beginning

I was born early in the morning in late February and joined my little donkey family. I could walk as soon as I was born. I remember drinking warm milk from my mommy until my tummy felt like it would burst. Then I would get sleepy and lie down on a grassy patch in the sun. Our family lived with a herd of cows inside a fence on a farm. There were lots of trees that provided shade, and there were little streams in the forest. There were also patches of grass in the warm sunshine.

My mom was beautiful with a very light-brown coat, almost blond. Her name was Lady. My dad was much darker and had big brown eyes that looked like they were outlined with eyeliner. His name was Gunny. They both had the pattern of a cross on their backs.

My dad had a deafening hee-haw when he was surprised or angry. I think he could be heard for miles away. Even though he was louder than my mom, she could be pretty fierce as well.

Once when my girl was running by our fence, she stopped and offered us some treats. Sometimes she gave us peanut butter crackers and sometimes apple cores. Her family was big, so they always had lots of apple cores to share. We loved apple cores because they were sweet and crunchy. Well, my mom became worried that I would not get enough treats. She must have thought Dad was crowding me. She pointed her backside toward my dad and started kicking. He looked surprised, but he quickly backed away before she hit him.

Our family spent all our time with the cows because we were all herd animals. That means that we all liked to hang out together. No one would like to be alone when they were meant to be in a group. It made sense to me that cows and donkeys were together. We all liked eating the same things such as grass and hay. We got along well with each other. As a group, we were stronger than horses, who got sick easily. There was one big difference between donkeys and cows though. We did not chew our cuds. That is one thing I never liked about cows. I thought it made more sense to chew your food and swallow it once. The cows liked to bring their food back up and chew it again. They had terrible breath all the time. One thing I never understood was that I had only one stomach and I only needed to chew once. They had four stomachs but needed to chew their food over and over.

I did enjoy playing with the baby cows. They were happy and silly and bouncy, just like I was. The mama cows were always serious and grumpy. They started to moo at us whenever we were running around. The baby cows were a little bit bigger than I was.

You see, donkeys come in different sizes. I am a miniature donkey just like my parents. We never get bigger than the baby cows. The mama cows are about three times bigger than we are. The bulls are even bigger.

Because my dad was so loud, sometimes I did not know if I should believe him or not. Once when I was young, I asked him why our family lived with the cows. He said that most donkeys lived with cows. This was the crazy part. He said that we lived with them to *protect* them. How could that be? The cows were *huge*! How could we protect them? My mom told me she would explain it when I was older.

Gunny

Lady

2

....

Learning about Life

At first, I could only drink milk from my mom when I was hungry. It did not take me long to figure out how to drink water and eat grass and hay.

When my girl was running, she often stopped just to look at me. I heard she even saw me the day I was born. When I was old enough to eat grass, she would get handfulls of it from the outside of my fence. She pushed her hands through the fence for me to nibble the green treat. The reason "the grass is always greener on the other side" is because my whole herd had already eaten the best grass on our side.

My mom taught me the best places to look for good grass. She also taught me which plants to avoid. My dad taught me how to swish my tail to drive away flies. When I was still young, they taught me one of my favorite things to do in the whole world. We were lucky to have a place in our pen that was just plain dirt. Nothing felt as good as rolling around on our backs with our legs in the air. All that dirt kept my coat fluffy and kept bugs away. My girl fussed at me a little bit, well, really just teased me, because I got so dirty. She said every time she patted me, little puffs of dirt rose from my coat. She was happy for me, though, because she knew I must have had a good day if I had a nice back-scratching roll in the dirt. I knew I looked silly, but it felt so good I wanted to squeal and giggle. It felt so good that I didn't even care if I looked crazy. The cows could scratch their backs on tree branches and fence posts, but we donkeys were just too short for that.

The noise my dad made was called braying. It seemed to me that girls could never be as loud as boys were. My dad had tried to teach me to bray, and I could definitely make some noise. The more excited I was, the louder my noise was. The problem was that my bray sounded more like I was crying or whining. I hoped that when I was older, my grown up hee-haw would happen.

3

....

A Donkey's Job

My parents told me a story once that happened before I was born. I think my mom may have been pregnant with me. She was pregnant with me for twelve months, an entire year. That was a really long time! Even though the cows were much bigger, they were only pregnant for nine months, just like people. Maybe it was because baby donkeys were born about half the size of adults and baby cows were born only about a quarter of the size of grown-up cows.

The story was about my girl walking one of her dogs. The dog's name was Sandy, and she was a teenager at the time. She was a long-haired yellow Lab who loved to bark and run. She took good care of my girl and was very protective. Normally, she was a bit clumsy and goofy, but never mean. No one knew what got into her on this particular day. As my girl was on the walking path beside our pen (called Aunt Marla's Driveway), Sandy bolted. She shot forward so fast and so strong that she jerked the leash from my girl's hand. She jumped through the fence and headed straight for my mom. At that particular spot of Aunt Marla's Driveway, the fence had three levels of barbed wire. Sandy left tufts of her golden fur in at least two places. Donkeys have never liked anything coming toward them, especially if that thing looked threatening. Sandy did. She was growling and barking fiercely.

The most powerful weapon that my dad had was his back kick. My dad started aiming at Sandy and must have kicked her. Sandy's threatening barks turned into high-pitched yelps of pain. My girl was outside the pen, screaming and crying for Sandy to come out. She didn't want anyone to get hurt. After Sandy got kicked, she went over to my girl who was holding the gate open for her to get out. She had her tail between her legs. My girl was scared because a donkey kick could kill a dog. She got Sandy back home and checked her out. Sandy had a little bit of blood on her face. She actually looked embarrassed but was otherwise okay. Maybe since Sandy was the biggest dog in her pen, she thought she could take on anything. Or maybe she thought she was protecting my girl. We would never know, but Sandy never got to go on leash walks on Aunt Marla's Driveway again.

4

....

The Big Move

I remember that day. It was the end of June on a bright and sunny morning. It was hot already. My girl had walked all around the outside of my pen looking for me. She was not by herself. She had her dad and papa with her. They found me and put me and my mom in a little pen. I felt that something important was happening. It felt scary and exciting all mixed together. They didn't let my dad come into the little pen. That made him start braying loudly. He never needed much of a reason to do that anyway. He was running around angrily. Probably my mom knew what was going on because she started telling me things. She said that I was a big girl now. She said that I was probably going to another herd of cows. She said that even if I didn't know it or feel it, I was a very brave donkey.

Apparently, I was supposed to get into a trailer. My girl's dad, who turned out to be my new farmer, wanted me to. My girl wanted me to. I did not want to. Donkeys can be very stubborn. When donkeys are scared, we simply refuse to move. The trailer was backed up to an open gate on the pen. I was pretty sure the farmer did not mean for my mom to come with me. How could I go by myself? I was just a baby donkey! Plus I was little since we were miniature donkeys. My mom must have known that this would happen soon since I didn't rely on her milk anymore. Even though she knew, she did not seem to like it either. She was braying a little bit, but she never sounded as loud or as angry as my dad. Finally, the farmer just picked me up and placed me gently in the trailer. He must have been strong. It did not hurt a bit. My girl was so excited, and I could tell she wanted me to be happy. She kept saying gentle and kind things to me. This did seem like an exciting adventure. Then the farmer closed the gate to the pen, and the trailer started moving. I was leaving my farm!

A truck pulled the trailer to the very next farm. We were close enough to my old farm for me to hear my mom calling for me. I answered her back as best I could. My bray was still not very loud, so it sounded like my mom was screaming for me to come home and I just sounded like I was crying.

Once we arrived at my new home, the farmer opened the door to the trailer. Even though I was excited, I did not budge. You see, part of our reputation of being stubborn is not true. Donkeys just deal with unknown situations by not moving. Since I did not know what was outside of that trailer, I froze. Once again, the farmer just squatted beside me and lifted me into his arms. He placed me on a grassy spot inside a fence.

My girl and her family called my new home Donkey Town. They always smiled when they said that. My new pen had no barbed wire for the fence, just squares. It had a big red barn. I had my own water bucket. Inside the barn, there was hay. There was no one else I had to share it with! It was incredible, but I was still sad. About the time I felt like a big girl with my own place, my mom would bray. She was checking on me. I brayed back that I missed her. It made me sad to think about her. She was sad too and missed me. When I got worried, I paced back and forth along one side of my pen. I even made a little path in the grass from all my pacing.

5

. . . .

Trudy the Curious Donkey

I still missed my mom, but my girl came out and brushed me every day. She gave me sweet feed in the morning and hay all the time. She still gave me treats too, and there was tall green grass in my pen. My girl told me that living in my new home meant I was growing up. After about a week, my mom stopped braying for me. Even though I still loved her, I didn't feel sad anymore. There were fun things to do in Donkey Town. My red barn was just for me and smelled like hay. That smell has always made me happy. It makes me feel like everything's okay, safe, and cozy. Sometimes I chewed on the wood in my barn. I could roll around on the soft dirt inside my barn.

My favorite things to chew on were my brushes. You see, my girl used to come out and brush me for a long time. It felt so good because I was always itchy! She used a metal curry comb that really scratched, and it got off all my loose dead fur. That curry comb had a bright-red handle, and I liked to pick it up and shake it. My girl thought it was so cute when I did that. She always tried to take a picture. Sometimes I just wasn't in the mood for a picture. Then my girl would use a dandy brush with red bristles set into a wooden handle. The bristles were rough and helped get off some of the caked dirt. I was always getting caked dirt on myself from playing in the mud. That brush felt good too, like a massage. She rubbed it over my muscles and then flicked the dirt off. Next, she used a body brush with soft bristles. This one smoothed my fur and made me look really pretty. She did this one on my legs and feet because it was gentle. Getting my little legs brushed felt the best, and I always tried to be well behaved and stand perfectly still. I didn't want her to stop because it felt so good. Donkeys have short manes that stand straight up. My girl told me that my mane was like a zebra's. I did not even know what a zebra was, so she told me it was a horse with black-and-white stripes. She may have been teasing me. I have never seen such a thing. Regular horses have longer manes that lie down. Since my mane stood straight up, she would brush it with a brush on each side and brush upwards, meeting at the top. My girl even liked to braid my tail. She was silly. Whenever she finished brushing me, she told me I was her favorite donkey and that she had always wanted to have a donkey. She also told me that I was beautiful. That made me feel happy on the inside.

There were other pens around mine. One fence was shared with bunny rabbits, and one fence was shared with dogs. The other was shared with my new herd of cows. The bunny rabbits fascinated me. I could stand for a long time just watching them hop around, like little blobs of fur. I would press my nose through the squares at the bottom of the fence to get closer to them. There were two bunnies, and they were named Luke and Leia. They were a brother and sister pair. They also ate grass like I did. The girl was bolder than the boy and would hop right next to the fence. She wanted to sniff me too! She hopped so close that our noses touched, and I could see her big brown eyes. Her fur was so long that it hung down over her entire face.

On another shared fence was the dog pen. When I first came to live in Donkey Town, the dogs didn't know what to do. They wanted to sniff me and would slowly get closer to our shared fence, then jump back. Then they would bark constantly. They did not know what I was. They barked at the cows too. I never told Sandy that I knew about her visit to my old farm. She never barked at me as if she planned to attack me. She just barked as if to let the family know that I was there. She also barked because she wanted to play. Simon was the most social of the dogs. He would come right up to me and stand on his hind legs to reach my nose. I would bend down and share a sniff. My girl loved it when we did this. She wanted everyone to play nicely.

I remembered that my dad had told me that cows needed donkeys. That still did not make sense to me. I had been so young at my old farm that I never really got to know the cows there. The cows at my new farm seemed nice enough. My girl and her sisters liked to name the cows. There was a huge bull they called Robert. There were five mama cows and three baby cows. There was one teenager cow named Cedar, who would become the next bull when he grew up. Robert was getting old. Even in his older years, Robert was a huge bull who was mild mannered and friendly. I was ready to start hanging out with the cows, but the farmer worried that I was still too little. So, for now, I just talked to the cows through my fence. My closest friend was Cedar, the bull-in-training. He always came over to my fence to talk to me. We would touch noses together through the squares of my fence.

Finally, that year in late fall, the farmer started letting me spend time with the cows. At first, I only stayed out with them during the day and had to come back to Donkey Town every night. That way my girl and the farmer made sure I was okay and got enough feed and water. The farmer teased my girl that she spoiled me, but secretly he loved me too. He said that I thought I was a dog. I knew I was a donkey. I couldn't help it if I loved to be petted and get treats! The farmer didn't want anything bad to happen to me with the cows in the big pasture. He knew how much my girl loved me.

It was wonderful being in the wide-open spaces of the pastures. There was even a pond on my new farm. On hot days, the cows would wade into the cool water and just stand there. I was so happy and carefree, I ran at a full sprint sometimes. There was not always a good reason, I just loved to run. Sometimes I tried to stop so far that I nearly tipped over. My girl called me her little race donkey. My girl was a runner too. She went running all over the farm on paths beside my fence, and I often raced right beside her. On the other side of my new farm was yet another farm. There were horses and alpacas there. The peacocks there were very loud and made spooky haunting sounds at night. There were goats there too that made bleating noises.

There was a tiny little opening from my Donkey Town into the cow pen. The cows were too big to squeeze through, so they couldn't eat my food. I could come and go as I pleased. If I ever got scared, I could always go back to my barn in Donkey Town. There I was safe and secure. One night, my girl didn't call me back to my pen. She let me stay out with the cows all night! I felt so grown-up. Just thinking about being grown-up made me happy, and feeling happy made me want to run.

6

· · · · · · · · · · · · · · · ·

Trudy the Mischievous Donkey

Just when I was doing great with the cows, the farmer made me go back to Donkey Town. It wasn't so bad at first, but then I got bored. After having a pond and endless pastures, my pen and red barn did not seem as big as they had before. Did I do something wrong? Was I in a donkey time-out? It made me feel grumpy. There was plenty of feed. There was a bucket of water. I said hello to Sandy and Simon. I watched Luke and Leia hop around. But I was supposed to be in a herd! Sometimes the cows came to the pasture outside my pen. Mostly, though, they spent all their time in a bright-green pasture down a hill from my pen.

Since I was cranky, I always nibbled on my girl when she came in my pen. Even though it made her mad, I had this way of leaning on her that nearly knocked her down. I would never really hurt her, but I would forget how heavy I was and how scrawny she was. I also liked to wrap my body around her so she couldn't escape. She always said, "No, Trudy, *stop*!" in her stern voice. She also said, "You're not a bad donkey, but you're making bad choices!" She wondered why I was cranky. She even worried about me. I heard her ask the farmer why I was so grouchy. Once when he was in my pen to feed me, I managed to nibble his work boots just right and I untied his shoes! That made me laugh and laugh.

During this time, I had a visitor. His name was Dr. Ed, and he gave me vaccines to keep me safe and healthy. Dr. Ed was a nice man, and he seemed to know a lot about animals. He even knew this trick of holding my head so that I couldn't move or bite him. It was a little aggravating, but I was impressed he could do that. He gave me shots, but I didn't even notice them. Dr. Ed was also nice because he knew just where it felt good to be scratched, like on my shoulders. I could tell he really loved animals. I overheard him talking to the farmer about keeping my hooves healthy. He said to be careful in the spring or whenever there is a lot of fresh green grass. Donkeys could get an infection in their hooves called foundering if they ate too much sweet grass. The farmer had already heard of that, and that's why I had not been with my herd lately.

I also heard them talking about something called deworming. A few weeks later, the farmer squirted some sweet apple-flavored juice in my mouth, which must have been my medicine for worms.

Once the cows had eaten all the new rye grass, I got to rejoin them.

7

. . . .

Trudy the Brave Donkey

With five mama cows and three baby cows, I knew we might get another baby. One morning another baby was born, and I was excited. She was able to walk right after being born, just like I did. Her mama licked her all over after she was born. She liked to sleep as most babies do. Sometimes her mom would tuck her behind a tuft of grass so that she could not be seen. It seemed the cows were always nervous about something getting their babies. Cows remained on high alert all the time, especially the mamas. Robert was the leader of the herd, but he often distanced himself while eating in other pastures.

The cows never really slept because they were always trying to look around for threats. I always felt that the mama cows thought I was silly and too young to be a genuine member of the herd. I wondered if those mama cows knew what my dad had told me about protecting the herd. I also remembered what my mom had told me, that I was brave even if I did not feel like it. I wanted to be all grown-up and useful. I wanted a loud hee-haw and a powerful back kick like my dad. I wanted my girl to be proud of me. But the only thing I knew I was good at was zooming. That's what she called it when I ran at supersonic speed. She said I was a zoomie donkey.

One night, the sun was beginning to set and we were all nibbling on grass in the pasture. Robert had gone up to a higher pasture as he often did lately. The mama of the newest baby had carefully hidden her and stepped off to eat more grass.

My huge ears heard a rustle in the woods between us and where she had left the baby. I couldn't explain this feeling I had, but all the hair on my mane stood straight up, and I felt angry and excited and worried at the same time. I turned around to face the noise and saw a coyote slinking quickly through the woods. Without even thinking about it, I started zooming as fast as my little legs could go. I shot like a rocket toward that coyote. All I could think about was blocking him from getting to that baby. The baby was still small and helpless, and even though she could walk, she couldn't run at all. I was trying to figure out how to get to that mean coyote and have time to back up to kick him before he reached the baby. But for now, I just kept zooming. It felt like I was flying without even telling my legs to move. The distance between me and the coyote was closing fast.

Then something incredible happened. From somewhere deep within my body, the loudest, meanest hee-haw I had ever heard roared from my mouth. It was so powerful that I felt like my lips were flapping in the force of it. It was as if my hee-haw went into automatic just like my zoomie legs. I charged toward the coyote, still unsure about how to use my back kick. But when he saw I was not scared of him and was charging toward him, he paid attention. He tucked his tail between his legs and ran away as quickly as he came.

I couldn't believe it! He ran away. I didn't even need to use my back kick! My lightning speed saved the day. I was useful! My mom was right when she said I was brave. I never even had time to think about what to do. I just did the right thing when I needed to.

I had never breathed that hard in my life. My heart was beating like a pounding drum. But I was also happy and relieved and proud of myself. My girl would be so proud of me! The only problem was that even though I could understand what she said by her tone of voice, she couldn't understand me so well.

The mama cow was mooing like crazy as she awkwardly ran toward the baby. She got to her and started licking her all over again just like when she was a baby.

Maybe that coyote knew he couldn't bother my herd when I was on the job.

8

. . . .

My Girl

The next time I saw my girl, I wanted her to know how brave I had been. I think she could tell I was a little more mature. Now it wasn't so silly that I was a zoomie donkey because that was maybe my superpower. It's what made me able to protect my herd. It's what made me special.

Once, for a while, my girl and her family stayed home all the time. They spent a lot of time outdoors, which was fun. We had a beautiful farm, so it was nice to have them outside more. One day, they had a picnic in the woods where I could join them.

I was so happy for them to be with me on my territory that I ran because of my excitement and joy. I ran supersonic speedy circles around them. They were laughing because I made them so happy.

I think now I know who I am. I am not a dog. I am not a cow. I am not a person. I am a donkey, a small, zoomie, and brave donkey.

The End

About the Author

Dr. Lori Langdon is a pediatrician who grew up on a hog-and-tobacco farm in rural North Carolina. She declared at age five on a hot summer day that she wished to grow up and become a doctor so that she could work in air conditioning. Through the years, she realized that her love of science and people would actually match that career. The Lord provided for her education with scholarships to NC State and then Duke University School of Medicine. After completing her pediatric residency at the University of Virginia, she and her family returned home to North Carolina. She married her high school sweetheart, Mark, and they now live on his family's farm. She loves her home church, Coats Baptist, loves entertaining, memorizing scripture, and international medical mission trips. She is a mother to six and a grandmother to one. She also loves her patients and their families. She believes life is a musical and loud spontaneous singing is perfectly appropriate.

CPSIA information can be obtained
at www.ICGtesting.com
Printed in the USA
LVHW021000241220
674974LV00011B/1022

9 781098 058227